Santa Where Are You?

by

Annette Phillip

The next few weeks are going to be so busy, I thought as I got ready for work. Then suddenly, my cell phone started ringing. I didn't expect the call until later. I reached for it on the table stand and answered.

"Hello! Elvina here, what's going on at the North Pole?"

Oh, just so you know, I am one of Santa's elves, disguised and stationed in an apartment building in NYC. I am responsible for getting all the naughty and nice lists in order before Christmas. I am in charge of receiving all the lists collected by elves based in different parts of the world, which I hand over to Santa so he can check them twice. New York City is our home-base office, which allows the elves easier and quicker access to me. We have two weeks until Christmas to get everything ready.

"Elvina, something is wrong. Santa is missing," said Wilfred, the Chief Elf of managing the portals.

"What happened?" I asked.

"He went through the portals for his practice run and never returned; we timed him like we normally do and he hasn't returned. This is not looking good," said Wilfred.

"I'm on my way. Open the portal to the North Pole."

When I arrived at the North Pole everybody was running around going crazy. This was unheard of. Santa has never gone missing, especially being so close to Christmas.

"Did you go through all the portals?" I asked.

"Yes," said Wilfred

The portal was one of our best inventions. It created a gateway that could send us to a place in seconds, which made Santa's trips go off without a hitch. He would deliver the presents on time through the chimney; this was still the original mode of delivering the toys. The portals made it easier to get to the countries without delay. An elf interrupted Wilfred, saying they'd noticed something different this time. Santa had been heading towards Sydney, Australia, then he suddenly diverted to another part of the country

The Mission: Save Santa!

Santa had headed into an area called Queensland. We sent elves through the portal to Sydney, Australia from there; they used a tracking device, which directed them to the forest in Queensland. The elves used Flying Fairy Dust we got from the fairies in Fairytale Land to get to

Queensland. They told us he went into the forest and the tracking device put them right in front of a very large oak tree, but they got no more signals after that. Their description of the oak tree and where it was located explained everything. Santa had ended up in Fairytale Land.

Fairytale Land was a place we had never ventured to before, however, we did have a business relationship with the fairies. It was a powerful and magical place, and most of the creatures and magical beings there were mischievous. We brought the magic of Christmas to the children here on Earth. The only other place besides Earth that Santa brought Christmas to was Whoville. It was located inside a giant snowflake, south of Mt. Crumpit in a place called Pontoons, which is in the South Pole. The "Whos", as they were called, were peaceful and loving creatures. It seemed odd that Santa would go to Fairytale Land, so close to Christmas. Something was definitely not right.

I turned and addressed the team of elves that helped Wilfred with the Portals:

"We have to go to Fairytale Land. Prepare a portal to Sydney, Australia."

Our relationship with the fairies in Fairytale Land started three years ago, two months before Christmas. They had heard about Santa Claus and his elves and the work that we did. They wanted the elves in the tailoring shop to design clothes for them. Our head elf designer Marlon was honored to work with the fairies. The fairies heard that elves could make clothes small enough to fit them, and they were excited, for no one in

Fairytale Land was experienced in such tiny tailoring. The fairies were about one to eight inches in height. They offered us their famous "Pixie Flying Dust" and "Blue Fairy Dust" in exchange for our fairy fashion services. Fairytale creatures didn't deal in human money. They instead chose to exchange goods for services. Santa had heard about the magical powers of Fairy Dust and realized how beneficial it could be to us. On that day, we officially started doing business with the fairies once a year. Blue Fairy Dust had many different magical powers; but it's main use was to get to Fairytale Land. The Blue Fairy dust was sprinkled on the middle section of the giant oak tree, which was the passageway that took you to and from Fairytale Land. The fairies had given us Blue Fairy Dust in case we ever wanted to visit them there.

Time is of the essence when you are Santa Claus. Here at the North Pole, we take our jobs seriously. We needed to find out what part of Fairytale Land Santa was in and get him back in time for Christmas.

Geared up and ready to go, we took the portal to Sydney, Australia, and brought the Pixie Flying Dust and Blue Fairy Dust with us. The Pixie Flying Dust was used if Santa needed the elves to get to places, to help out other elves, or to make the trips faster and easier after we arrived using the portals. We planned on traveling at night, as to not draw too much attention to ourselves. This was an adventure we never expected.

As night approached, we used the Pixie Flying Dust to fly from Sydney to Queensland, Australia. I took six elves with me and we had a couple of elves on standby at the North Pole in case we needed further assistance. We were unclear of what we were about to undertake, so the more elves we had the better. When we got to the oak tree in the forest, one of the elves sprinkled some of the Blue Fairy Dust on the center of the tree. It opened up the passageway into Fairytale Land; we cautiously went in not knowing what awaited us.

Fairytale Land was new to us. From the stories the fairies told us, it was known to be an enchanted forest full of fantastic forces and beings such as goblins, fairies, gnomes, the Three Little Pigs, Red Riding Hood, evil queens, witches, and all kinds of other mythical creatures. The forest can be a place of enchantment, danger, and magic they told us. They said to expect the unexpected. So there was no surprise that we had no idea what part of the enchanted forest we had arrived in.

We noticed an old frog hopping by and decided to ask if he knew where we were. Talking to a frog was not unusual in this neck of the woods.

"Hi, Mr. Frog. My name is Elvina, Chief Elf of Santa's Workshop," I said

"Hey 'croak.' Oh! I've heard of Santa Claus. I didn't realize he came to these parts 'croak.' I thought his magic was only used for the children of Earth," he said.

"How can I help you? I'm in a bit of a rush," he said.

The frog claimed he was looking for a princess, any princess, to kiss him because he was really a prince. He was cursed by Maleficent, the evil queen of curses. He had to kiss a princess to change back, and he didn't have time to chat.

"Are you by chance a Princess?" he asked me.

"No I am not," I chuckled. "We just got to Fairytale Land, and have no idea where we are. Could you kindly tell us where we are?"

He told us we were in the land of Prince Charming and Princess Cinderella. We asked how to find the castle and he directed us. The castle was located on a hill with a flight of stairs and he told us to be prepared for a little extra walking.

He said the prince might not look as charming as before, and that we would soon find out why. Flying Pixie Dust to the rescue! We flew in the direction of the castle.

We approached the castle and heard a lot of loud banging and stuff being thrown all over the place. The knocker was so gigantic, I thought I would never be able to lift it. I gathered all my strength and I knocked on the big, brown door.

"Who is there, and what do you want?" someone yelled from inside.

"Hi! We are a group of Elves from Earth's North Pole. We are looking for Santa Claus, and we think he might be in Fairytale Land." I said.

Prince Charming opened the door and shouted sarcastically,

"Do you *see* any Santa Claus around here?"

I had to ask him, "What's wrong? Aren't you Prince Charming, married to the kind and gentle Princess Cinderella?"

He really didn't look charming at this moment. His hair was disheveled and his eyes were puffy like he'd been crying all night. He smelled so awful that I didn't think he had showered for many days. We had to back up a bit when he came close. The smell was pungent: What had Cinderella done to Prince Charming?

"Cinderella!? Cinderella the Cinder and Ashes woman, left me for the cursed beast that is married to Belle. They live in the Chateau de Chambord in the deep forest not too far from here."

> He continued by saying, "She heard the Beast was loaded and he knew how to really charm the ladies; something he learned from me by the way."

"She didn't find me charming anymore, and left me for that hairy beast!"

Prince Charming said she lived by the fireplace when he met her, and he brought her back from the brink of poverty and abuse by her two stepsisters and Stepmother.

"The shame of it all!" he said and broke down in tears.

"He now has two beautiful women. I knew we shouldn't have gone over there for those dinners. I always wondered why Cinderella was always flirtatious. She was getting it on with the Beast!"

We all stood in stunned silence. How were we going to ask him for help?

After that meltdown, we had to come up with something. I carefully addressed the Prince, "On Earth, there is something called a dating app that allows you to meet people. You meet a lot of beautiful women and eventually you find the woman of your dreams."

I *was* stretching it a bit. But I told him that if he helped us find Santa Claus, we would put him on something called an "App" to help him meet women. I promised him he could meet women all day long and soon Cinderella would become a distant memory.

I explained that he had to get his act together and become Prince Charming again if he was to win the ladies' hearts. I also gave him the names of some of the apps.

He looked at some called Tinderella, MatchHer.com, and, the most popular, Plenty of Females or "POF". He was happy and intrigued and decided to check them out right away.

Prince Charming, elated at his success, then gave us a bit of information. The Prince said that he had been to the Sleeping Beauty antique shop, and had overheard Snow White's stepmother mentioning to someone that she "didn't know any place they could put "The Present". She continued to say that she would ask her mirror on the wall if there was a good location to 'hide him.'

Prince Charming said at the time he didn't pay any attention as she was always up to something ever since Snow White had turned on her.

We asked Prince Charming for directions to Snow White's stepmother's castle. We had heard stories of Snow White's stepmother, the queen, forcing Snow White to run away in fear for her life.

Her stepmother was really an evil queen, with many magical powers, including a magic mirror. The stories also said she was very vain and was very jealous of her stepdaughter. It was as if Snow White's beauty was detrimental to the queen's very existence somehow. She wanted to be the only beautiful queen in Fairytale Land and her magical mirror gave her an update every day as to who was the fairest of them all. Snow White was obviously more beautiful (hence the Queen's hatred).

I could understand Snow White fleeing from this mad and evil Queen. To approach her, we had to think fast. I came up with an idea I thought would work on someone so self-centered.

I had a couple of the elves head back home, and they came back with some beauty products from Sephora. They also brought with them the Timewise Face Cream Day and Night for Mature Adults from Mary Kay. That would be appropriate for someone so vain. Evidently, the mirror couldn't help alter the Queen's appearance but only judge it. Prince Charming told us the Queen's castle was about ten miles from his castle.

Flying Pixie Dust was needed to travel the distance as it was dark and too far to walk.

When we arrived at the front of the castle, it was medieval and dark at the top of a hill. We saw a courtyard and noticed the wishing well where we were told that Snow White spent most of her time. We read some of the stories, so we had an idea of their character backgrounds. We headed up the stairs and knocked on the heavy door.

"What's with them and these heavy doors?", I wondered aloud.

A very weird and ugly dwarf opened the door. We told him that we needed to speak to the Queen urgently. He was reluctant to let us in, but we insisted that it was urgent and beneficial to his Queen.

"Modrick! Who is there?" someone inside the castle shouted.

"Weird looking elves, claiming to be looking for someone who doesn't live in Fairytale Land, Your Majesty."

She entered, still regal with a cold look on her face which was now covered with wrinkles. Worry had visibly aged her and I could tell that she would definitely need the face creams and makeup we had brought for her.

"Is it about Snow White? Did she return to Fairytale Land all poor and haggard? " she asked, smirking.

"These are elves looking for their missing Santa Claus. They think *you* might have an idea where he is," Modrick said grumpily.

We explained to her who Santa was and how someone had told us they overheard her talking about a mysterious "present" in the antique shop.

"Why would I give you such information, and what's in it for me if I do?" the queen bellowed, "If you elves don't leave right now, I will zap you into tomorrow."

I thought to myself, in this place anything can happen, so we panicked and quickly presented her with our gifts.

"Your Majesty, if you can help us by sharing the information you received about Santa's whereabouts, I guarantee that I have beauty products that can make you look beautiful again," I explained.

In full detail, I told her all about the products, and I decided to apply the cream and makeup to her face. When I was done, she looked into her mirror and asked it who was the fairest of them all.

The mirror said, "You, of course! You are the fairest of them all, Your Majesty. It has been a long time, but I think you are back!"

Her face lit up and she said, "Eat your heart out, Snow White!"

After her transformation, she was more than willing to help us. She explained that the Big Bad Wolf had come to her and said he had a relative visiting and wanted a place for him to stay. She said she would ask the mirror where there was a cottage available. When she mentioned the mirror, the wolf changed his mind and said he would ask the Three Little Pigs.

"I guess he didn't trust my mirror; after all, it has a reputation around here and that wolf was sneaky. I'm sure he thought the mirror would expose his secret plan." She chuckled at that.

"I was curious about his relationship with the Three

Little Pigs, as they were not exactly friends. But who knows what goes on these days?" she said and shrugged.

We thanked her and I gave her instructions on how to use the beauty products so that she would always look beautiful. She then provided us with directions to the Three Little Pigs home. When we arrived, we were blown away (no pun intended). They had a huge and elaborate mansion that was almost as big as a castle.

We were told that after two of the Pigs' houses got blown away by the Big Bad Wolf, they went into the real estate business. "Good for them," I thought. They would finally have that wolf stop blowing away their houses. As usual, we knocked on a heavy door, this time the door was made of solid gold. The knocker was out of this world. It was made of bronze and shaped into three pigs with gold embellishments (no surprise there). After two knocks, a male pig butler opened the door with an unfriendly look. We asked to see the pigs and again explained why we had come there.

With a loud, unfriendly snort, the butler said he would be right back and had us wait in a grand foyer.

A few minutes later, the Three Little Pigs appeared with the butler at their side. The Three Pigs moved in unison. I told them my name was Elvina, Chief Elf of Santa's Workshop, and we were presently looking for him. They said they had heard of him and that he went down chimneys.

They couldn't figure out how a big belly guy squeezed down those small chimneys. The Pigs said they would love it if they could try, and they started squealing. I guess it is a pig's way of laughing.

Wilfred bellowed, "Can you help us or not? We are running out of time!"

They told us that the Big Bad Wolf had come to them asking if they would rent him their guest house on the west side of the mansion, for a dear friend of his that was visiting. The Wolf lived not too far from the pigs mansion, but his place was too small. They noticed something strange in the Wolf's pickup truck the day he came to ask them to rent the guest house. They saw something moving in the back that looked green and had a wide Cheshire smile.

"We wondered why he would ask us in the first place, given our history," the Pigs continued. They said that after he blew up their homes and they got the mansion, he realized he couldn't blow their houses down anymore so he gave up the fight. He was in the marijuana business now, since selling marijuana had recently become legal in Fairytale Land.

He was too busy to bother with the Pigs anymore. The same pigs who said that they didn't want to be around the Wolf anyway. Unfortunately when he got high, which was often, he would go on and on about all his problems, which was something The Pigs wanted no part of.

"The Wolf and Prince Charming are good friends. Charming would go over to Big Bad's place and they would smoke all their problems away," said one of the Pigs.

"Very pathetic if you asked me. They both have women issues. Don't see how they can help each other with that," the other Pig chuckled.

He continued by saying, "Charming and his Cinderella issues, and Big Bad who was juggling two She- Wolves named Sheila Wolfer and Beatrice Wolfin."

The third Pig chimed in by saying, "Big Bad told us the she-wolves were becoming dangerous for him; he couldn't make up his mind which she-wolf he wanted, hence the drama."

The Pigs shook their heads in unison. They did the Wolf favors so he would be nice to them, they said. Judging from that, I figured they had rented him the guest house. Turns out, I was right. The Pigs told us that two nights ago, when the wolf decided to move into the guesthouse, they heard a lot of commotion and peeped out the window. They saw Big Bad and a green hairy, pot- bellied, pear shaped, ugly looking thing.

They had three huge, red bags and the green ugly thing appeared to be pretty strong, as he carried two of the bags on his own. The pigs said they noticed one of the bags was moving but couldn't make out what was inside.

"That's the Grinch. That snake! He is trying to steal Christmas again, this time he is stealing Santa too. We have got to stop them!" I shouted.

We thanked the Three Little Pigs, said goodbye ,and told them we would be back in a couple of days. We then decided to head back to the North Pole to discuss how we were going to free Santa from these two goons. At the North Pole, all of Santa's elves were disturbed by this turn of events. Christmas was fast approaching and we had to work fast to get Santa back in time.

As Chief Elf, I told the other elves to gather anything we could use to help make this escape plan work. One elf suggested we get leaf blowers to target the Big Bad Wolf. The idea was to have him blown far, far away. I told the elves to get ropes and chains because restraining the Grinch would be somewhat difficult. I had a suspicion that the Grinch's heart had gotten smaller from the looks of things. The Grinch was known to have a heart two sizes smaller than the average heart and because of that, he was a mean creature. He lived in a cave alone close to the village of Whoville. One Christmas he heard the Who's celebrating; they were known to be very cheerful and happy people. He got annoyed and decided to take away their Christmas. A little girl by the name of Cindy Lou was the one who helped save their Christmas that year. She befriended the Grinch and showed him the true meaning of Christmas and what it meant to her village. The love and happiness caused the Grinch's heart to grow two sizes bigger, making him happy and full of cheer, like the Whos. Evidently, something went wrong between then and now because that heart had definitely shrunk.

It took a couple of days to get everything ready for the great Santa Christmas escape. We arrived the same way, through the portal, and flew by way of Flying Pixie Dust to Queensland into the great big oak tree. This time we had no problems getting to our destination and we headed straight to the home of the Three Little Pigs. We arrived at about one o'clock in the afternoon. The Pigs told us the Grinch and Big Bad Wolf went out for dinner around three in the afternoon every day. There was a three o'clock lunch special at Red Riding Hood's diner and bar, they called it the Red Hoodie.

We had two hours to get our plan in order and head out after they left. We gave the Three Little Pigs walkie-talkies to let us know when they left, and when they were about to return. We didn't want to take any chances. This trip, I took a small team of elves that were trained in elf combat, three combat elves, three that were with us on the first trip, and me. In total there were seven of us; we had to be prepared for anything. We are small creatures, only about three feet in height, so we needed strength behind us. Santa was also an easy target and having elves trained to get him out of danger was of utmost importance.

We didn't know for a fact if the Wolf and the Grinch had

Santa, but from the description the Three Little Pigs gave, and given the time of year and the Grinch's involvement, we were not taking any chances. He hated Christmas and would do anything to destroy it. We had to start somewhere and this plan sure made sense. The Three Little Pigs told us we could use one of their old houses. The Pig that had built his house of bricks, which Big Bad Wolf couldn't huff and puff down, still owned it. He said it was abandoned and that it was a five-minute walk away from the mansion. The Pigs said they were going to restore it and use it as a shelter for unfortunate Pigs in need. Even Fairytale Land had broken homes! This was where we would get ready before we launched Operation Rescue Santa.

> The Three Little Pigs didn't want any part of this. They had come a long way and tried to stay on the good side of the Big Bad Wolf, so they opted out. They gave us the directions to the abandoned brick house, told us good luck, and went inside their mansion. The only thing we asked of them was to alert us with the walkie-talkies.

When we got to the Brick House, we started sorting out the stuff we brought. We had ropes and chains; the chains were for the Grinch as he was a very tall, strong, pear-shaped creature. We brought three leaf blowers because the Pigs explained how powerful the Wolf was when he huffed and puffed. We needed blowers that had more strength to blow him far away. Flying

Pixie Dust would be used also. We were small compared to Big Bad and the Grinch; flying would give us an advantage because we could corner them easily. The elves in the North Pole were on alert in case we needed backup, and by backup, I meant Cindy Lou, the little girl from Whoville who had helped change the Grinch that Christmas. She knew how to get that small heart of his to grow two times bigger. If our plan didn't work, we would surely need Cindy's help.

We all dressed as warrior elves. We had full leather armor and medieval vests strapped with warrior cuffs. A couple of the combat elves brought swords. The Grinch and the Big Bad Wolf would wish they had never taken Santa. One of the Pigs came in on my walkie-talkie to tell us that the Grinch and Big Bad were leaving for the diner, and we should move now.

"This is it, guys! We grab Santa and run. If by any chance they get back before we get out, we will be ready for them," I said.

The three combat elves and I would head to the guest house to rescue Santa. The other three elves stayed in the brick house with the leaf blowers, rope, and chains. The plan was to get Santa out before they returned. We started heading to the west side of the mansion, towards the guest house.

There was a small flower garden and a nicely mowed lawn in that area of the mansion. Not too far from the flower garden was a wooden Pavilion Gazebo, oval-shaped with a single roof. The Pigs were definitely living in style. The guest house was situated just up in front of the gazebo. As we started approaching the guest house we heard loud talking. At first, we thought the Wolf and Grinch were back, then we heard loud laughter. A Ho Ho Ho belly kinda laughter and right away the elves and I knew that was Santa.

Why is Santa laughing? I thought. We decided to break down that door. One of the combat elves had a crowbar, which we used to open the door.

As soon as we opened the door and rushed in, our jaws almost hit the floor. Santa was relaxed and sitting on the couch watching TV, and a big bowl of salad was in his hands. He looked somewhat different but at that moment I couldn't tell what it was.

"Santa! "I shouted, "We came to rescue you! Get your bags and let's get out of here before the Wolf and Grinch get back."

> Santa looked at me and said, "Elvina! Elves! Come sit down and watch TV with me. I just finished watching Bad Santa and I'm about to watch Bad Santa 2. It's hilarious and only on Netflix instant play. I had a Smart TV in one of my Christmas bags and got it out so the boys and I could watch."

My eyes and ears almost popped out. Did I hear and see correctly or was this a bad dream? I would soon find out.

"Santa, you were kidnapped by these two goons. Why would you not want to leave right now? The elves and I came to rescue you." I said, looking shocked at Santa's inaction.

Santa told us to sit down and he would explain everything. He told us that he really had been kidnapped. When he first got here, he was angry and tried to escape and he wanted to get back to the North Pole. He asked the Grinch why he kidnapped him. Santa thought the Grinch had grown to love Christmas. The Grinch explained he wanted to get back at Santa for skipping last Christmas at Whoville. He said the Whos were like family and were very disappointed Santa didn't show up, especially Cindy Lou.

The Grinch had gotten angry and his heart shrank back to two sizes smaller. He made a plan to kidnap Santa, so he would see how it felt to miss Christmas. The Grinch also wanted to disappoint the children on Earth, the way the Whos were disappointed last Christmas. Santa told us he explained to the Grinch that it was an oversight on his part, that he concentrated so much on the children of Earth that he forgot the Whos. Santa said he knew that Whoville was the only other place he brought Christmas to and it's not that he thought they weren't important, he just put more emphasis on the children this year.

The naughty list was getting longer every year and he had hoped that when the naughty children didn't get any gifts this year, they would learn a lesson and that would change the outcome of the naughty and nice lists for next year. I did agree with him on that point; I had noticed this year we had many more naughty children than we had nice ones.

I asked Santa how the Grinch and the Wolf kidnapped him in the first place. He explained that the fairies also did business with the Whos, and they visited Whoville where they were introduced to the Grinch. The Whos explained how the Grinch became a better creature after they showed him the true meaning and happiness Christmas brought. The Grinch then became friends with the fairies who extended an invitation to him to visit Fairytale Land anytime he wanted. He took them up on that offer and would frequent the place often.

Santa went on to say that when he missed Christmas at Whoville, the Grinch had gotten really upset and vowed to get his revenge. The Whos had no idea what the Grinch was up to. It was on one of his visits to Fairytale land that he became friends with the Big Bad Wolf. The Grinch had overheard the fairies talking about Santa's test runs and how impressed they were. That's when the Grinch and the Big Bad Wolf began planning their kidnapping and it started with the knowledge that Santa was heading to Australia so they would ambush him in Sydney.

"After they caught me in Sidney, they brought me to Fairytale Land. They thought it would be the perfect place to keep me because not many of the folks in Fairytale Land know much about me," Santa said.

"Wow Santa! That story was crazy! Payback is horrible," I said.

Santa told us that after he explained and apologized to the Grinch, he and the Big Bad Wolf were nicer to him. He said being in Fairy tale Land gave him perspective and he had to take a hard look at himself and his job as Santa. He didn't like his Santa look anymore, especially his extra round belly. It made him Jolly Santa, but right now he hated it.

He also said that he was discouraged because there were such a high number of naughty children this year but he had forgotten that the Whos should have tipped the scales more to the nice side since they were the nicest creatures he had ever met.

He decided to start dieting right away and the Big Bad Wolf told him about Whole Foods Supermarket owned by Shrek and Princess Fiona. The couple had just been visiting her parents in the Kingdom of Far Far Away. While they were there, they ate a lot of foods rich in carbs, fats and sugars. By the time they got back home to the swamp, they almost couldn't fit through their doorway. That's when they decided to go on a diet and open the Whole Foods Supermarket.

'The Guys', as he called them, encouraged Santa to buy his food from this same market. He was amazed at how much weight he had lost already. He said he actually enjoyed the wholesome foods. Santa explained to us that he needed to take a sabbatical, he wanted to lose some weight, and focus on some other projects. He told us that he had started writing and was thinking of publishing a book sometime next year, and he would definitely be needing this Christmas off.

I was blown away by this sudden rush of news and looked at the other elves in disbelief. Some shrugged their shoulders and some shook their heads.

"But Santa what are we to do?" I asked. "Christmas is a few days away,".

Santa smiled and said, "Elvina, you are the Chief Elf. I know you will figure out what to do. I believe in you!"

Just then, the door opened. Evidently, the Three Little Pigs were trying to reach us on the walkie-talkies but we were so distracted by Santa's news that we didn't hear it. In walked the Grinch and the Big Bad Wolf. They didn't look surprised to see us. They figured we would try and rescue our beloved Santa Claus because Christmas was only days away, so it was only a matter of time before we would show up. They didn't prepare to fight and neither did we. At this point, after hearing Santa's big news we were not sure that we had the strength to fight anymore.

Santa told the Grinch and Big Bad that he had explained everything to us about his decision to stay. But he promised the Grinch that no matter what, the Whos would get their

Christmas.

"Santa I would like to apologize again for my behavior. I would like to say to you and your elves that this will never happen again," the Grinch expressed sincerely.

"Thank you for not hurting our Santa, Grinch. We accept your apology, and like Santa, said we would definitely make it up to the Whos." I said.

The Big Bad Wolf came up to Santa and asked if he could talk to him some more about his girlfriend troubles because the talk they had the night before had really helped. He needed to make a decision and wanted Santa's opinion. Santa gave us a wink and told the wolf he would be with him shortly.

Then he came over to us and said, "You elves are the best. I know you can save Christmas without me. You got this! I will be back but I just need some 'me time'."

"Santa don't worry, we will get all the presents delivered to the children and the Whos. We will miss you, but take as much time as you need," I said

I hugged Santa and told him to contact us when he was ready to come back. It seemed like there was nothing else we could do to change his mind. When all of a sudden, an idea popped into my head.

"Let's get out of here, elves. We are going to save Christmas,"

I said.

Back at the North Pole, Christmas Eve had arrived and everyone was full of energy. Getting the reindeer, sleigh, and toys ready was a big deal.

"Elvina, everything is ready to go," said Wilfred.

I was elated. There was no Santa this year but I had devised an ingenious plan to save Christmas without Santa.

Allow me to explain: when we left the guest house, I got an idea. I thought, why don't I ask the Three Little Pigs to be replacement Santas? Time was running out and having three of them in different parts of the world would help us bring all the presents to the children before it was too late.

I spoke to the other elves and they thought it was a brilliant idea. We went straight to the mansion to ask the Pigs if they were in and they said yes right away. They said they needed a break from Fairytale Land and they were excited to see how they would fit down a chimney with their fat bellies; they wanted the 'Santa experience.'

We brought the three pigs to the North Pole where they were debriefed as to their official Santa duties. The elves in the training department started working with the Three Little Pigs immediately. They showed them how to go through the portals from one country to another in the time allocated and how to get down and up the chimneys before they were seen by anyone.

The chimneys were truly the highlight of the Pigs' Santa adventure. They just loved it. The elves in the tailoring department made the perfect Santa suits that outlined their little round bellies.

Lessons with the elf vocal coach helped with "Ho Ho Ho's" because we had to ensure they didn't snort until after Christmas. By the time we were done working with them, the Three Little Pigs were perfect little piggy Santas.

As promised, we had the Three Little Pigs head to Whoville to bring the Whos their presents. This time around we would definitely not forget them. Santa even had us give double the presents for the Whos to make up for not getting any the year before.

The Whos visited us after Christmas and they were so happy with the presents that they thanked us profusely. They told us the Grinch had explained what he had done and apologized for the trouble he caused everyone.

They understood why he did what he had done and they forgave him for it. They also weren't really upset with Santa because they understood the burden he carried, each year working tirelessly trying to get presents to everyone in the world on Christmas Day. We told The Whos that we would tell Santa that they had visited and promised that we would never forget them at Christmas again.

Santa took that year off to write his book "How to Use Christmas Spirit to Fix Your Life". It was picked up by Pinnocio's Publishing and was soon at the top of the best sellers list. Due to the notoriety he earned from the book he began seeing some of the Fairy Tale Land residents for counselling sessions. Prince Charming, Cinderella, and the Evil Queen were some of his most notable clients. Keep an eye out for his follow up book "Ho Ho Hold Me! *Using Christmas Spirit to Learn the Art of Vulnerability*"

MERRY CHRISTMAS!

From Santa's Elves.

THE END